PUPS
SAVE A
TRAIN

PaRragon

Bath · New York · Cologne · Melbourne · Delhi
Hong Kong · Shenzhen · Singapore

Chase and Rubble are tidying up the Adventure Bay sandpit. Rubble fills it with new sand, then makes a sand bulldozer for the children.

"Wow, Rubble!"
says Chase.
"What can I say,
I'm a builder pup!"
says Rubble.

Meanwhile, Katie and her cat, Cali, are on the train home from Katie's grandma's house. Cali reaches for a bag on the seat.

"Sorry, Cali," says Katie. "Grandma made these treats for the PAW Patrol."

Suddenly, the train starts shaking. There's a rockslide on the track and the train has to stop.

Katie calls Ryder for help.

"The PAW Patrol is on the way," says Ryder. "No job is too big, no pup is too small!"

Rocky, Marshall, Zuma and Skye are playing
football when their Pup Tags light up.
"PAW Patrol, to the Lookout!" calls Ryder.

All the pups rush to the control room and line up in their uniforms. "PAW Patrol is ready for action, Ryder, sir!" says Chase.

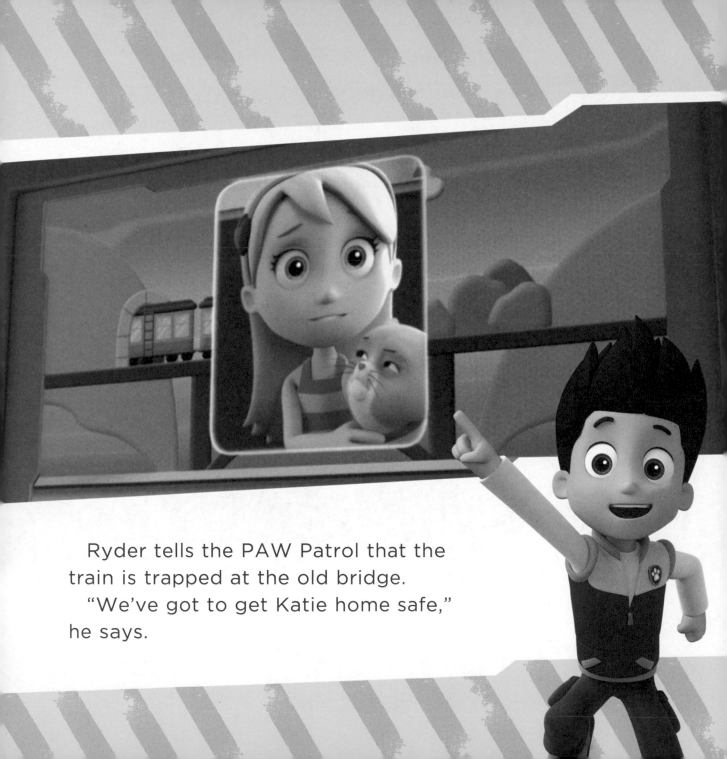

Ryder tells the PAW Patrol that the train is trapped at the old bridge.

"We've got to get Katie home safe," he says.

Ryder needs Rubble and his digger to scoop up the rocks, and Rocky and his garbage truck to take the rocks away.

"Let's dig it!" says Rubble.

"Green means go!" barks Rocky.

Ryder, Rubble and Rocky zoom to the bridge at top speed. Meanwhile, Katie peers out of the train window to look for her friends. Suddenly, she sees them.

"Ryder and the PAW Patrol are here, Cali!" says Katie.

But Cali has spotted a seagull outside. She climbs out of the window to follow it onto the roof.

"Cali," Katie calls. "Come back!"

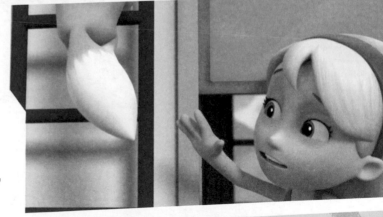

Ryder and the pups look all around,
checking that the train tracks aren't broken.
"The tracks are okay," says Ryder. "We
just need to clear the rocks so we can get
the train off the bridge!"

"Rubble on the double!" barks Rubble. He uses his digger to scoop the rocks into Rocky's truck.

Ryder hurries down the hill to take a look at the bridge. "Rocky!" Ryder says through his helmet mike. "A beam has cracked. If it breaks, the train will fall."

"We can prop up the bridge with a log," says Rocky. "But my truck won't be able to carry it down the hill – it's too steep!"

"We need an extra set of paws," says Ryder.

Back at the Lookout, the other pups are watching the rescue on the screen. Just then, Ryder appears.

"Chase, I need you and your truck at the bridge as soon as possible," says Ryder.

"Chase is on the case!" he barks and jumps into his police truck.

When Chase arrives, Ryder and Rocky
are tying a rope around an enormous log.
"Hi, Chase," says Ryder. "We need your winch
to lower this log down to the bottom of the
bridge. We'll use it to hold up the broken beam."

Chase attaches the rope to the winch.
Then Rubble uses his digger to push
the log over the edge of the hill.

At the bottom of the hill, Ryder and Rocky
move the log into place.

"That's perfect," says Rocky. "It will hold
until we get the train off the bridge."

Just then they get a call from Katie on the train.
"Cali is missing," she says.
"Don't worry, Chase will find her," says Ryder.

Cali is on the roof of the train, hoping to steal some bread from the seagull. Suddenly, the cat slips.

"Meow!" she cries, hanging on with just one paw.

Luckily, Chase spots her between the carriages. "Cali, I'm here to help. Just take my paw."

Phew! The PAW Patrol has cleared the track and Cali is safe, too. The train can get moving again.

Later, Katie, Ryder and the PAW Patrol are playing in the park.

"Thanks, Ryder, thanks PAW Patrol," says Katie, giving the pups their special treats.

"You're welcome," say the pups. "Whenever there's trouble, just yelp for help!"